JACKSON JONES AND THE CURSE OF THE OUTLAW ROSE

Also by Mary Quattlebaum

Novels
Jackson Jones and the Puddle of Thorns
Jackson Jones and Mission Greentop
Grover G. Graham and Me
The Magic Squad and the Dog of Great Potential
Jazz, Pizzazz, and the Silver Threads

Picture Books
Winter Friends
Aunt Cecee, Aunt Belle, and Mama's Surprise
Underground Train
A Year on My Street

JACKSON JONES
AND THE
CURSE OF THE
OUTLAW ROSE

•••••••••••••••••••••••••••••••••

MARY QUATTLEBAUM

Delacorte Press

Published by
Delacorte Press
an imprint of
Random House Children's Books
a division of Random House, Inc.
New York

Visit us on the Web! www.randomhouse.com/kids
Educators and librarians, for a variety of teaching tools, visit us at
www.randomhouse.com/teachers

Library of Congress Cataloging-in-Publication Data
Quattlebaum, Mary.
Jackson Jones and the curse of the outlaw rose / Mary Quattlebaum.
p. cm.
Summary: When Jackson and Reuben take a rose cutting from a
graveyard for Mr. Kerring, events make them believe it is cursed and
will continue to threaten anyone in its vicinity until it is returned.
ISBN: 978-0-385-73349-6 (trade) — ISBN: 978-0-385-90365-3 (glb)
[1. Blessing and cursing—Fiction. 2. Roses—Fiction.
3. Community gardens—Fiction. 4. Gardening—Fiction.
5. Single-parent families—Fiction. 6. African Americans—Fiction.]
I. Title: Curse of the outlaw rose. II. Title.
PZ7.Q19Jabc 2006
[Fic]—dc22   2006001804

The text of this book is set in 12-point Bookman Light.

Book design by Trish Parcell Watts

Printed in the United States of America

November 2006

10 9 8 7 6 5 4 3 2 1

BVG

To Anne D.,
friend, poet, and green-thing grower

CHAPTER ONE

• •

Light barely crept through the gray trees. The damp ground sucked at my shoes and a breeze slid past my neck.

I slapped at a bug.

"Shhh," whispered Reuben behind me.

"What do you mean 'shhh'?" I whispered back. "Nobody can hear."

"We're in a *cemetery*." Reuben's voice dipped lower. "We need to show respect."

I turned. "I *am* showing—"

Next thing—*ow!*—I hit the ground.

"You okay?" Reuben whispered.

"*Quit* whispering," I said very loud. "It's making me nervous."

Reuben shot me a scared look. "Man, look what tripped you."

I struggled to my feet. "Stop it, Reuben," I said. "I bumped into a gravestone, that's all."

Beyond the old cemetery, the dark forest rustled. "Let's go, Jackson." Reuben's voice cracked. "Something's out there."

"We need to get what we came for," I replied, edging past the moss-slick gravestone.

Then I saw the name cut in that stone.

Rose Cassoway.

Behind the grave, a thorny rope of flowers twined round a broken fence.

Roses. I should have known roses would do me in.

A chill grabbed my whole neck.

• • •

Roses have always brought me bad luck. But thanks to my mama, I am stuck with them—and all their little green cousins: African violets, philodendrons, pansies. Mama loves plants. Our home is stuffed with them. This might be fine in the country, where Mama grew up, but it is way too much green for a city apartment. I eat with a fern, sleep in a jungle, talk to a six-foot ficus.

Whenever I complain, Mama smiles. She claims plants are good for you. Her words: "They clear the air, soothe the eyes, and decrease stress."

Decrease stress. That's a laugh.

This past year has been the most stressful of my life.

Right to that very moment in the graveyard.

It all started on my tenth birthday last April. I had been sure I was getting a basketball. But Mama gave me . . . dirt. A plot in Rooter's Community Garden on Evert Street. And there was no way I could give it back. Mama had been so happy to give me a "little piece of country."

Talk about trouble. That garden constantly messed with me. And my puddle-of-thorns rosebush was the worst. My best bud, Reuben Casey, and I spent all summer trying to grow *something* (besides weeds). Then I spent all fall trying to save the garden—my plot and twenty-eight others. I rescued Rooter's from certain doom, from being bulldozed and turned into a building.

Now it was April again. I needed a break from plants.

Instead, they were still in my face. Literally.

That's because Mama had gone back to college to study plants. And she had started her own business, Green Thumb. Two days a week she tended the green things in offices; the other days she worked a normal job downtown. Green Thumb now had twelve clients, and Mama's business was growing. Literally.

Well, I just started my own business, too. I have only one client—but he feels like twelve 'cause he keeps me so busy. Mr. Kerring is my next-plot neighbor at Rooter's. He is the oldest and bossiest person I know. The man can remember back to when Rooter's was a World War II victory garden, more than sixty years ago.

Mr. K. was the very reason I was standing

that day in a cemetery. Shivering by a grave. Staring at roses.

Crackle-crick. That noise again from the forest. Closer this time. Reuben's eyes widened. "Jackson," he whispered. "What do you think—"

CHAPTER TWO

•••••••••••••••••••••

"*Quit* whispering." I grabbed the rose vine. "It's probably a squirrel."

"Or a bear."

I pulled some teeny scissors from my pocket.

Reuben snorted. "You gonna trim the bear's toenails?"

"For your information, these are house-plant *pruning* shears. I'm gonna take a cutting. Here, hold this end."

Reuben cautiously pinched the vine. "Tell me again why we're doing this."

"Because Mr. K. wants to be a rose rustler."

Of course, right then the man was waiting

in a rental car by the side of the road. And Reuben and I were stuck in the cemetery.

As I opened the shears, I got a sudden mind picture of how our rustling had started. Two days before Mr. K. and I had visited Rooter's, and the man, as usual, had begun bossing his plants. Commanding them to grow. Then he'd started in on *my* rosebush.

"Late spring already and not one single bud."

Now, my rosebush was no sweet-blooming angel, believe me. It was a puddle of thorns. A mess of mean sticks. But last fall it had snagged a bully named Blood. Laid him low. Since then, well . . . I might not like roses, but I have *respect*.

Mr. K. had pointed to the yellow blooms climbing Rooter's chain-link fence. "*Those* are roses," he'd said. "Tough as cowhide." He had banged his cane for emphasis. "My gran brought the clipping from Texas, stuck in a potato. Those roses have survived drought, flood, and heat that would singe your hair. No coddling for them. And they flower longer than any modern fancy-pants rose."

Mr. K. had banged his cane again. It stuck in the garden path.

I had helped wrestle it out. "Thanks, Jackson," he'd sighed.

Even more than today's puny roses, Mr. K. hated his cane. He had always worked his own perfect plot, but last winter he had taken a bad fall. So he had hired me to bend and lift and tote. My job: to keep his plants marching in straight rows.

That day in Rooter's, he had proposed another job: rose rustling.

"We'll search abandoned houses," he had explained, eyes gleaming. "We'll hunt in graveyards. I used to rustle roses all the time when I was younger. That's how you find bushes more than a hundred years old."

"Why don't you just *buy* a rosebush?"

"The old roses are hardier and prettier, and smell sweeter, too. But people don't grow them anymore, so stores don't stock 'em. All you can get are big show-off hybrids. No, you have to hunt for the old ones. With rustlin', you never know what you might find."

Rustling, huh? Sounded like Mr. K. wanted

to play outlaw of the Old West. Cowboy hat and all. I was hoping he'd forget the whole idea in a week.

The man had shuffled down the path to his grandmother's roses and carefully snapped off a few. "For your mama," he said. "Isn't that your car?"

"Car" didn't exactly describe what Mama was driving. It was huge, hulking, and green.

The zucchini mobile. Mama's van for her Green Thumb business.

But at least it was big enough to hold me, Mr. K., the cane, and all Mama's snipping, sprinkling, plant-doctoring tools.

"Those roses smell wonderful!" Mama greeted us. "And what unusual petals. What are they called?"

"They don't need any fancy-pants name," Mr. K. humphed, climbing into the van. " 'Rose' is good enough. Right, Jackson?"

"Uh, yeah," I said, slouching low in my seat.

As Mama steered the zuke mobile up Evert Street, I slouched lower. Up ahead was the blacktop, a basketball net, and four hoop-shooting guys.

It was impossible to hide.

As the zuke mobile cruised by, each guy grinned and stuck up a thumb.

For Green Thumb.

Talk about embarrassing.

In one year, Rooter's had *crushed* my cool reputation. Believe me, I am no Farmer in the Dell. One blacktop-booming, b-ball ace, that's me. Shootin', jukin', always on the move. Dribble, dunk—SCORE.

I got a sudden mind picture of me in a cowboy hat. A rose rustler rather than a basketball star. I shuddered. Surely, Mr. K. would forget.

● ● ●

But the old man had been struck by rose-rustling fever. He talked and planned, and before we could say no way, no how, he was driving Reuben and me to a country graveyard. He had read a newspaper article about developers discovering a cemetery in a stretch of woods, with markers dating to 1842. Since folks back then planted flowers by graves, he was sure we would find some old roses.

And we had, twined round the grave of Rose Cassoway.

"Rustling is *stealin'*." Reuben's whisper shivered through the cemetery.

"No," I explained very slowly and for the fourth time. "Rustling is just a word. These old roses are public property, Mr. K. says. Anyway, we're not going to dig up a whole bush. We're just taking a cutting."

"From a *graveyard*," Reuben said.

"You afraid some ghost will jump out?"

Reuben didn't crack a smile. "Remember Nemo Comic Number 2? When the Flawt stole the golden orb from the emperor's tomb. Remember the curse?"

"That was made up!" I said. "*We* made it up. This is real life. There aren't any curses. Anyway, that was an *orb*, we're only taking a little twig."

"I just . . . don't . . . know." Reuben's voice trailed off. "Hey, let's go home and finish our new Nemo strip."

I sighed. Persnickety, careful, and poke-turtle slow—that was Reuben. Every Captain Nemo he drew, he eyeballed and erased. Every b-ball he threw had to be carefully aimed. The boy *tiptoed* into adventure.

But we've been best friends since first grade, creators of Captain Nemo Outer-Space Comics since third. And now we were rose rustlers.

I tried to joke Reuben out of his worry. "Wooooo," I moaned, flapping my sleeves. "I am the ghost of Rose Cassoway. Who dares touch my precious rooooooses?"

"Wooo all you want," Reuben said. "I still think it's wrong."

"Woooooooo." I clicked my shears.

"Shhh," Reuben said sharply. "What's that?"

"It's Rose Cassoway, of course." *Snip.* I neatly cut the vine. The small piece fell.

Crackle-crick.

Something grabbed my shoulder.

CHAPTER THREE

• •

"Aargh!" I screamed.

The grip tightened.

"Please," Reuben whimpered.

A voice spoke: "What in the . . . Sam Hill are you doing?"

The voice didn't wail. It didn't moan. And what kind of ghost said "Sam Hill"?

Cautiously I peeked over my shoulder.

A bearded man smiled at me. "Sorry to scare you boys," he said, dropping his hand. "I didn't want you getting too close to that fence."

Reuben and I stepped back.

"I manage the clean-up crew for the housing development in the field close by," he explained. "We've got orders to cut all the growth in this abandoned cemetery, then tear down that old fence and put up a new one. You know, tidy things up a bit. The job should take one day, two at the most. But the strangest thing . . ." The man shook his head. "The crew yesterday got poison ivy. *Bad* poison ivy. Must have been some on that fence."

"What about you?" I snuck a glance at his hand.

"I wasn't here." The man squinted at the fence. "Came to check out the situation today."

I squinted, too. I'd recognize poison ivy anywhere, thanks to all the fields I'd tromped in with my plant-loving mama. *Leaves of three, let them be.*

"Huh." I squinted harder. "I don't *see* any poison ivy."

"Neither do I," said the man. "That's what's so strange. And this isn't the season for it. The only way I can figure, maybe the guys had a reaction to those flowers."

On the fence, the little roses swayed.

Reuben shivered. "See, Jackson?" he whispered. "The curse."

"Curse?" the man asked.

I squirmed. "My friend here thinks that, well, taking something from a graveyard—"

"Brings on a curse," Reuben finished. "You gotta show respect."

"Curses only happen in movies or books," scoffed the man. "I tell you, this is nothing but carelessness. With bad luck thrown in. When Jake broke his leg—"

"Was he close to the fence?" asked Reuben.

"Yeah," said the man. "He tripped over that gravestone."

Reuben crossed his arms. "Just like you, Jackson."

I crossed my arms right back. "Reuben, you gotta stop all that woo-woo talk *now*. You're scaring yourself."

Reuben snorted. "Wasn't me screaming."

"I yelled."

"Screamed," replied Reuben. "Like a girl in a horror movie."

"Yelled."

"Okay, okay," the man broke in. "Yelled, screamed—you made a noise." This time he squinted at us. "You two jumped like a couple of outlaws."

I squirmed again.

"Yeah," said the man. "Like a couple of out-laws . . . caught doing wrong."

"We were just taking a cutting." I picked up the fallen rose twig.

"You two gardeners?" asked the man skeptically.

"Sort of." I sighed, thinking of my puddle of thorns at Rooter's. "We're getting this twig thing for a, um, friend. Anyway, these roses are public property. We're not breaking any laws."

"Still doesn't make it right," Reuben muttered.

"We gotta go," I said to the man. "Our friend's waiting."

"He driving the getaway car?"

I pictured Mr. K. behind the wheel of the Datsun he'd rented. He had started bossing that car the moment he stepped on the gas.

"Come on, I'll walk you out." The man smiled at me. "Don't want any more yells—or screams." He fished an empty candy wrapper from his pocket. "Wrap that stick in this paper. It'll protect your hand against thorns and a possible rash."

As we filed past the other graves, I glanced back once. In the shadow of Rose Cassoway's stone, the tiny pink roses gleamed. The cutting shifted in my pocket.

"Broken legs, poison ivy, bees." The man shook his head. "At this rate, we'll never remove that fence."

"Bees?" Reuben asked.

"Got stung myself the other day," said the man, striding down the path. "Huge bee swooped out of nowhere, buzzing like a jet. That's why I wasn't here yesterday. My arm swelled big as a cantaloupe."

Reuben gasped.

"Don't even start," I said firmly. "Bees *sting.* That's what they do. It has nothing to do with a curse."

CHAPTER FOUR

● ●

Three days later Reuben was still repeating his graveyard words.

He was a kid with a two-word vocabulary.

The curse. The curse. The curse.

"I tell you, Jackson," he muttered darkly. "The curse."

"It's a whatchacallit . . . *coincidence*," I said. "Mr. K. just happened to fall."

"*And* sprain his ankle," said Reuben.

"Well, that other guy broke his leg."

"People keep getting *hurt*. Like in Nemo Comic Number 2: The Curse of the Golden Orb."

"Oooh, and now we're in The Curse of the . . . the Outlaw Rose, dread flower of the

18

Old West. Reuben, my man, lighten *up*." I gave him a poke.

Why did Reuben have to ruin a nice after-school walk to Rooter's with all his doom-and-gloom talk? Three days before, we had given Mr. K. the graveyard cutting and he had happily taken it home. And yesterday, that's right, he had fallen. But a tumble could happen to anyone, especially a guy who banged his cane. Mr. K. had lost his balance, that's all.

We had just visited him at his retirement home. Mr. K. had taken a break from bossing his nurse to ask if I could take the cutting to Mama to root. "This bum ankle," he had explained sadly, "will keep me from getting the right soil."

How could I say no? I carried the cutting, wrapped in wet paper towels, out of his building. On Evert Street, I raised it high on my palm, like a waiter in an ooh-la-la restaurant.

I stopped at Rooter's chain-link fence to take in the garden. The twenty-nine plots were showing new green shoots. And Mr. K.'s old-time yellow roses were blooming.

"I got a bad feeling," Reuben said, all jumpy. "Why you gotta bring that thing to my building?"

"Well, *your* building also happens to be *my* building," I pointed out. Reuben lived in Apartment 316; I lived in 302.

And here came our neighbors from Apartment 506. Juana Rivera and her too-loud sister and brother. Gaby, age seven, and five-year-old Ro.

"Shhh, no more curse talk," I murmured to Reuben. "Nothing about outlaw roses. We don't want to scare the little kids."

Like me, Ro carried something in his palm.

Like Reuben, Juana and Gaby regarded it grimly.

"You got a present for me?" I grinned at the little guy.

"Meet my worm!" Ro proudly introduced his wiggly pet.

"Disgusting." Gaby shuddered.

Juana hunkered down beside her brother. "Why don't you let the worm go," she suggested. "I bet he misses his friends."

"*I'm* his friend," Ro pointed out. "I'm

protecting him. If I let him go, a bird might eat him."

"How you gonna take care of him?" Gaby asked.

"Mailbags will show me," Ro announced.

Not that Mailbags was a big fan of worms, but he did know a lot about gardens. The man was always grubbing in his plot at Rooter's, growing zucchini and beans. And Mailbags lived in our building, too. Apartment 102. Ro didn't have to travel far for expert advice.

Gaby tried another strategy. "That worm is not even a 'he,'" she said. "It's a he-she. Male *and* female."

Ro's eyes widened. "Cool," he breathed.

We all bent closer to the worm.

That's when a big hand shoved me. And lifted the wrapped cutting from my palm.

I stumbled into Ro.

"Jackson," the little boy cried. "You're squishing my worm."

From behind me came a voice.

"What's this, Rose Jones? Your little sweet pea?"

Blood Green.

Blood was the meanest kid in the city, maybe on the whole planet. And that boy was BIG. Plus, he had strategy. He never smacked, hit, or taunted when adults were around. No, Blood waited till it was him against some scared kid. Then he let you have it.

All last year he had talked trash about me. Rose Jones. Farmer Boy. Pansy.

Then one day last fall it was me and him. Alone at Rooter's. When he jumped, I thought that was the end.

But he missed me—and tangled with my puddle of thorns. Literally. He got caught and stuck by my fierce pile of sticks. I had worked him free—on one condition. If he made fun of me, Reuben, Juana, or the little kids again— ever again—I would tell the whole school he'd been beat up by a rosebush.

His promise had lasted till he caught sight of Mama's new zucchini mobile. Now he called me Pickle, too.

Blood tossed the cutting high in the air.

"Come and get it, Rosey," he brayed.

"Give it back, Blood," Juana demanded. To me, she whispered, "What is it?"

Blood caught the cutting. Tore at the wet paper towels.

"Um, Blood." Reuben watched nervously. "You might not want to do that."

"You gonna stop me, Art Fart?" Blood sneered. He waved the bit of rose twig. "Oh, a bitty wittle stick," he cooed.

That boy dropped the twig on the sidewalk. Lifted his big foot to stomp.

Bzzzz. I swear the sound came from nowhere. *Bzzzz.*

A huge bee zoomed by. Zeroed in on Blood. Stung him, right on the cheek.

Blood screamed.

"The curse," whispered Reuben. His voice was filled with awe.

CHAPTER FIVE

• •

We watched as Blood, still screaming, tore down the street.

Slowly I retrieved the cutting. Rewrapped the paper towels.

Reuben opened Rooter's gate and steered me inside. "Jackson," he said, "we gotta decide what to do."

Juana was suddenly alert. "What do you mean?"

Reuben scuffed his shoe on the wood-chip path.

"And why," said Juana, "did you say 'the curse' like that?"

"Like what?"

"All spooky and mysterious."

"It's nothing, Juana," I said. "Reuben's just a little . . . worried."

"You think that was a coincidence?" Reuben looked straight at me.

"*What* was a coincidence?" Juana shook Reuben's arm.

"Okay, tell me this," I said to Reuben. "How come nothing has happened to me? I was the one did the cutting." I held out my arms. "Look, no poison ivy. No bee stings. No broken bones."

"I don't know," Reuben said slowly. "Maybe it's saving your punishment. Maybe you'll get it *bad*."

He glanced sideways at me. "Or maybe you're like your mama."

"What do you mean?"

"Well, Mailbags says she has a gift. She can talk the puniest flower into growing. He says plants just plain like your mama."

"So?"

"So, maybe they like you, too. You might have inherited, you know, that gift. Maybe it's protecting you."

I sat down slowly. "Reuben," I said, "that is the craziest thing I ever heard."

"What's crazy?" Juana glanced from Reuben to me. "What's protecting you? If you don't tell me, I'm . . . I'm going to throw Ro's *worm* at you."

"No," howled Ro.

"Then spit it out." Juana glared at us.

"Gaby and Ro might get scared," Reuben said. "This is sort of a ghost story."

"I *love* ghost stories." Gaby plopped down beside me.

"I'm never scared," Ro declared, cupping his worm.

So Reuben and I told how we had visited the cemetery and taken the rose cutting. Reuben's voice got all spooky and mysterious, talking about the bee stings and poison ivy and broken legs.

"Mr. K. sprained his ankle," I corrected. "He didn't break his leg."

"An ankle is part of your leg," Reuben replied. "His leg got hurt."

Juana regarded me. "I take it you don't believe in this curse."

"*What* curse?" I said. "The bee stings, the broken leg, the sprained ankle—those things just happened. Bad luck and carelessness. That's what the clean-up guy in the grave-yard said."

Ro started to cry. "I'm scared."

"Here, *querido*." Juana took him gently by the arm. "Let's find some dirt for your worm."

Ro sniffled.

"You can put the dirt in my pockets," Gaby offered. She followed them to a far-off plot and started to dig.

Shadows gathered in the garden as the sun started setting.

Reuben and I continued to sit.

No, I did not believe in the curse. On the other hand, I'd always had bad luck with roses. And if I had inherited my mother's gift, as Mailbags called it, someday I might find myself studying plants. Tending to plants. Even . . . talking to plants.

I squeezed my eyes shut. Drew a mind picture of me on the blacktop. Dribbling, shooting, scoring. Time after time after time. I was an ace at basketball, not flowers.

When I opened my eyes, the first thing I saw: those old-time yellow roses. Those Texas roses waving from Rooter's fence. The wrapped cutting was damp in my hand.

Reuben was gone, helping with Ro's worm home. I could hear voices and laughter.

No, I did not believe in the curse.

But roses had always brought me bad luck.

CHAPTER SIX

•••••••••••••••••••••

We straggled home, with Ro riding me piggy-back and Gaby carting dirt in her pockets. Reuben dogged my every step with doom-and-gloom sighs. When we reached our building, he headed for his apartment. His grandma, Miz Lady, was waiting. Or maybe he wanted to put some distance between himself and the cutting.

The rest of us knocked on Mailbags's door.

"A fine pet," the man pronounced when Ro flourished his worm. "The perfect size. Won't eat much or take up much room."

Mailbags himself takes up a lot of room. If the man jumped, I bet he could touch the ceiling. The worm was a skinny noodle beside his buffalo self. As for eating, huh. Mailbags has come to our place for dinner. Whole zucchinis disappear.

Yeah, Ro's worm was in good hands. Mailbags even had a whole book on the creatures. Gaby pulled the dirt out of her pockets and dumped it in a plastic cup. Then Mailbags handed Ro a bit of banana.

The boy raised it to his lips.

Mailbags laughed. "That's for your worm," he said. "A little fruit twice a week and soon your pet will be fat as a tire."

Gaby gasped.

"I'm kidding," Mailbags said. "But watch, that worm will consume the banana and pass it through. In a few weeks, Ro will have the richest dirt around."

"You can have it for your garden," Ro promised.

"What about your worm?" asked Mailbags, walking us to the door.

"I'll get him more dirt and he can start again." Ro waved good-bye. "He's going to live with me forever."

"He-she," muttered Gaby as we moseyed to the elevator. "And I don't want him-her living near me."

I was about to step into the elevator with the Riveras, when I remembered the cutting. I'd left it at Mailbags's. That stick looked a lot like trash. What if he'd thrown it away?

"Wait, Jackson." Mailbags trotted out to the hallway. Handed me the soggy paper towel. "You're looking wrung out, my man. Bad day?"

I didn't want to get into the whole curse thing. "Can I ask you something? About my mama?"

Mailbags looked surprised. "Maybe."

"You've said she has a gift, a way with plants." I rushed the words out. "You told her she should go back to college—"

"Wait a minute," said Mailbags. "I don't see *me* telling your mama what to do. She made up her own mind."

"Well, you gave her the college catalog."

"A small thing."

"Anyway, that gift she has. With plants." I

glanced up at him, then down at my shoes. "You think I have it, too?"

"Ah," Mailbags said. "The green-thumb gift." He considered my question. "Not sure yet what I think, but this is what I see: a boy who's on the blacktop more than at Rooter's."

"That what you see?"

Mailbags nodded. "That boy, he's a quick dribbler. But come planting? Oh, he's sloooww."

I felt relief course through me. "So you think b-ball is my gift?"

Mailbags palmed my head. "That boy is fast on the court. Got lots of fancy moves. Course, he *could* use some work on the hoops."

"Hey!" I grinned, punching the elevator button.

"This boy, the one we're talking about—"

I stepped into the elevator.

"Well, he does have a way with . . . weeds." Mailbags winked. "For him, they grow big as sequoias."

I continued grinning as the elevator shot up. Huh, that Mailbags. Mama was always saying how we kids bugged him. Asking this and that, following him around. "A full-time mail job and night college, too"—she'd shake her head—"the man doesn't have time to breathe, and you kids dogging his heels."

Wait till Mama heard about Mailbags and the worm house.

When I opened the door, Mama gave me a hug and immediately felt my forehead. "You feel okay?" she asked. "You look tired."

Yeah, well, a curse (even if it's not) can wear a boy out.

I wiggled away and held out the cutting. "Can you root this for Mr. K.?"

"How's he doing?" she asked, settling the cutting in a pot.

"When Reuben and I stopped by, he was bossing his nurse."

"Then he's feeling better." Mama laughed. "When he's quiet and mouse-meek, that's when I worry."

Mama checked several small bags of soil, chose one, and tucked its contents round the cutting. "This little guy will soon feel good about growing and start putting out roots," she said. "Pick a spot at Rooter's with good sun. You can probably transplant in a few weeks."

I watched as Mama gently touched the cutting. Mama and Mr. K. sure treat their green things differently. Mama chats to them softly, encouraging blooms. Mr. K. barks them into bigness.

"Mama," I said suddenly, "do plants have feelings?"

She turned to me in surprise. "Not feelings like humans," she said slowly. "And yet . . ." Mama brushed her cheek, leaving a dirt smudge. "Plants seem to *sense* the feelings of other species and respond. Scientists have done studies."

"What kind?"

"Let's see, they've discovered that plants tend to withdraw and wither in places with shouting and loud noises." She smiled. "But other scientists claim these studies prove nothing."

"So plants can't really get angry, right? They can't, you know, take revenge?"

"Only people seem to do that." Mama paused. "Sometimes, though, I can sense what a plant might need—different light, more water. And I try to help." She laughed a little. "As you know, the plants sometimes respond so well that the green takes over. . . ." She waved at our living-room jungle. "Hey, why this sudden interest in plant feelings?"

"Just curious." I hesitated, then touched the cutting myself. It was a little stick. An ordinary twig.

Nothing to worry about. I was just jumpy from Reuben's doom-and-gloom curse talk.

CHAPTER SEVEN

• •

For the next few weeks, the cutting sat peacefully on the window ledge in the kitchen. I pictured roots forming, tiny white shootlets. A little stick, doing what it should. An ordinary twig.

Blood, though, was the opposite of peaceful.

The boy prowled the school halls. He shoved and tripped kids. Nothing new about that. But his right cheek was puffed like a blowfish. All his insults were slurred.

"Flower Boy" came out "Sshawa ba." Kids giggled at his taunts.

Talk flew around school. Blood would be

puffy from that bee sting forever. The swelling was getting worse. No, it was better. The doctor had told Blood all he could do was wait.

The boy's eyes were two narrow slits in his fat-cheek face. Seeking out Reuben and me.

Not for the first time, I puzzled on Blood. Why was he so mean?

I had tried avoiding the boy, talking to him, even hitting back. My rosebush had stuck him good.

Nothing had worked. His meanness had gotten worse. Name-calling, punching, stealing. Maybe Blood had never learned such meanness was wrong. That it was flat-out wrong to hurt others. Even in kindergarten, when he had been Howard instead of that dumb name, Blood, he had given himself, he had tormented littler kids.

While Blood prowled puffy and the cutting perched peaceful, Ro's worm grew bigger and BIGGER and BIGGER. Ro carted that worm house EVERYWHERE. He murmured through the holes in the plastic lid, like a business guy on his cell phone. And that worm? It would waggle its skinny head out of the dirt, as if chitchatting with a friend.

Ro had to move his pet to a bigger house, a plastic bowl. And still it grew. Bigger and BIGGER and BIGGER.

Finally, Juana asked an important question: "Is that worm eating too much?"

We were sprawled on the steps of our apartment building. The whole world smelled clean, washed by a recent rain. Grass blades waved from sidewalk cracks. Sparrows dipped beaks in small puddles. Most likely, the weeds in Rooter's were growing as big as Ro's worm. I knew I should mosey to the garden and see.

"That worm's a monster," Gaby declared. "Wormzilla."

"He's healthy!" Ro clutched his bowl.

"Wormenstein."

Reuben nudged me. "Maybe Ro has a gift, like your mama."

A *worm* gift? All I can say is, if that boy's gift was as powerful-strong as my mama's, then Juana and Gaby were in trouble. I had just escaped my apartment, where Mama's gift was in full force. She was planning her Green Thumb display for the city's big garden show in a month. The show took place every year in the convention center, she had told me. It was the best place for landscape artists and plant businesses to advertise.

"Advertise" usually means a sign, right? Maybe a TV commercial.

Not at this show. Some businesses created entire gardens inside. Fountains, trees, five kinds of flowers. Even waterfalls. Green Thumb did not have that kind of money, Mama told me. She would create a small, modest display.

Small? Modest? As she experimented with different designs, Mama turned our whole apartment into one HUGE ever-changing garden display. She kept moving the ficus, hanging signs, arranging flowerpots.

Too much plant chat! I had escaped my too-green apartment . . . to listen to Ro and his worm.

Reuben poked me. "What about *your* gift?" he asked. "Seen any poison ivy or huge bees lately? Broken any bones?"

"Were you talking to me?" I poked back. "The guy with the slam-dunk gift? For your information, that cutting has been as peaceful as any of Mama's plants. An ordinary twig."

I jumped up. "In fact, that thing should be ready to plant now at Rooter's."

All the joking went out of Reuben. "Let's bring it back to the graveyard," he urged.

"I know the perfect spot at Rooter's." I ignored his doom-and-gloom tone. "Come on, we'll surprise Mr. K."

"Can I bring my worm?" Ro piped up.

"Sure, we'll take him on a field trip," said Juana. "Get it? *Field* trip?" She glanced at Reuben's serious face. "Never mind."

"Ro!" Gaby roared, dusting her jeans. "You spilled worm poop on my pants."

"Soil," Ro corrected.

Reuben rose slooowwwly. "I'll go with you," he said, all poke-turtle cautious. "But I still think it's wrong."

I stomped through the door. I wasn't going to listen to Reuben's gotta-have-respect speech *again*.

I fetched the little stick, got transplanting instructions from Mama, marched everyone down to Rooter's, and stuck that thing in the ground.

I'm not saying that what happened next began at that moment. Or that the cutting caused it. I *am* saying that a change occurred.

I would call that change a coincidence. Unlike doom-and-gloom Reuben, I would never call it a curse.

CHAPTER EIGHT

· ·

From that day on, the city got hotter and HOTTER and HOTTER. Ninety degrees, ninety-three degrees, ninety-seven degrees. And the rain stopped falling. It was the hottest, driest May on record. Water was rationed. Mama took a quick shower only every other day, so we could save water for her plants.

In our apartment, the pansies, primroses, philodendrons, and ficus survived. Outside, the green things shriveled and turned brown. Grass blades disappeared from sidewalk cracks. We had to set out bowls of water for the thirsty sparrows.

Rooter's looked as sad as one of Reuben's lost planets. Even Captain Nemo wouldn't have been able to save it. All twenty-nine plots looked pitiful. Even the weeds shriveled. And my rosebush? My fierce puddle of thorns? It drooped like the weepiest willow.

Now, a drought is a drought. Nothing supernatural about that.

But here comes the strange part.

In its perfect place by the fence, close to Mr. K.'s roses, sat the transplanted twig. The thing didn't grow or die. It stayed exactly the same. But around it—and this was *really* strange— those small Texas roses bloomed. The only bright patch of color in the brown garden. Maybe the only roses growing in the city.

"Must be the soil," I told Reuben when we stopped by the garden after school. There was no sound from the blacktop on Evert Street. No shouts. No quick-dribblin' *bounce-bounce-bounce*. The blacktop had been empty for days. No one could play b-ball in the heat.

"Probably a lot of worms by those roses," I went on. "You know, making that rich worm-poop dirt." The heat shimmered around the yellow flowers. "Anyway, roses like sun. They can't grow in shade."

I scratched at my sweat-soaked T-shirt. "Mr. K. said those old-time roses were tough," I continued. "Remember how his grandma stuck a cutting in a potato?"

"Jackson." Reuben took a deep breath. "I got an idea for a new Nemo villain."

"Go on." I was surprised. I was the idea man on our Nemo team. I wrote; Reuben drew. That's how we had worked for years.

Reuben scuffed at the sidewalk. "This bad guy is . . . invisible."

"Invisible?"

Reuben crossed his arms. "A ghost."

I stared at him. "What gave you *that* idea?"

Reuben gazed out at the yellow roses.

"So you're saying Rooter's is haunted?"

Reuben was silent.

"And a ghost is tending those flowers?"

"They're blooming, aren't they? And everything else is dying."

"But we've never *seen*—"

"What you expecting, Jackson?" Reuben snorted. "A floating sheet?"

CHAPTER NINE

• • • • • • • • • • • • • • • • • • • •

Well, I don't have much experience with ghosts and restless spirits. They belong in dark mansions and crumbly castles. *Not* in a city garden. Halloween is ghost time. The other 364 days of the year, they should stay put.

Reuben and I checked out the Internet. We visited the library. We found lots of stories about ghosts. Mean ghosts and kind ghosts. Foggy ghosts you could see and chill-breeze ghosts that you couldn't. Some broke vases and pushed people. Some drifted up and down stairs. One smelled like lavender, another like paint.

There was nothing about haunted plants. Or ghosts that liked to tend roses.

But one Friday after school we found a battered book with a brown cover at the library.

"It must be a hundred years old," said Reuben, gently turning the brittle pages.

"Phew!" I held my nose. "Talk about musty."

The book was full of the usual ghost stuff: ghost ships, ghost pirates, ghost ladies who wept. But it did have one important chapter: "How to Banish Ghosts."

Reuben and I read that chapter twice. Then we sat silent, thinking.

Finally my man cleared his throat. "You gotta communicate with it, Jackson. Find out what it wants."

"Me?"

"You're the one who took the cutting." Reuben pointed to a sentence in the book. "You 'interfered with its natural sphere.'"

"But listen to this." I read another sentence aloud. "'Be prepared. Contact may infuriate the ghost.'" I drew out the word: "In-fur-i-ate. What if it destroys the garden?"

Reuben shook his head. "I don't think this ghost is mean. It's just—well, something's not right. That's why you've got to communicate."

Communicate. I got a sudden mind picture of me talking to empty air. "All right," I grumbled. "But don't tell Juana and the kids what we're doing. Don't tell *anybody*."

"Yeah," said Reuben. "We don't want to scare them. And if something goes wrong . . . Well, we don't want the ghost to transfer its energy, like the book says. To start haunting someone else."

Reuben replaced the ghost book on the shelf. "Let's go."

"Now?"

My man squared his shoulders. He looked like Captain Nemo on a mission.

Mission: outlaw rose.

We marched out of the library, up the street to Evert, past the empty b-ball blacktop.

A ghost. I was about to talk to a ghost. My hands were sweaty—and not just from the heat.

What if the ghost got mad? Started throwing things? Followed us home?

I shivered.

We marched right to Rooter's gate, then stopped. Reuben glanced at me. I wiped my palms on my shirt. Lifted the latch.

Stepped inside.

In its place by the fence, close to Mr. K.'s roses—the garden's only flowers—sat the transplanted twig.

Someone knelt beside it. I saw a mound of dirt. A flash of silver.

"Nooo," I screamed, rushing forward.

CHAPTER TEN

• • • • • • • • • • • • • • • • • • • •

I hurtled through plots. Stumbled over a shrub.

The figure whirled. I saw a face. Another flash of silver.

Ro dropped his spoon and burst into tears.

"What happened?" Juana and Gaby raced from the other side of the garden. Juana grabbed the little boy. "What's wrong, Ro? Who screamed?"

Sobbing, Ro pointed at me.

"I didn't *scream*," I said, panting.

"You did! You did!" Gaby hopped about.

"Jackson *scared* me," Ro howled.

"Shhh, it's okay." Juana patted his back, frowned at me. "Why did you scream at Ro?"

"I *yelled* to make him stop digging."

Gaby sniffed. "He can dig. It's a free country."

"He can't dig there."

Juana stiffened. "That's not your plot, Mr. Guard of the Garden. Ro's just looking for another worm. He'll put back the dirt."

"My worm needs a friend," Ro blubbered.

"Okay, Ro, okay." I tried to soothe him. "I'll help you. Let's dig in Mailbags's plot."

Gaby sniffed again. "There won't be any worms in that hard ground." She swung her arm round the whole brown garden, then pointed at the yellow roses. "This is the only place where things are growing."

"That's why—"

"Shhh," warned Reuben.

"What?" asked Gaby, suddenly alert.

"Nothing," said Reuben.

"Nothing," I said.

"Tell me!" Gaby stomped on my toe.

"There's nothing to tell."

Gaby shot me a sly look. She picked up the silver spoon. "Come on, Ro."

She poked at the ground.

"Don't," said Reuben sharply.

"Why not?" Gaby chopped away with the spoon.

That girl would infuriate the ghost for sure. What if it drifted up like fog? Started haunting her? It would serve Gaby right if she got poison ivy or a broken leg or a bee-stung puffed-up face.

"Dig, dig, dig," Gaby sang. She chopped closer and closer to the transplanted twig.

"Stop!" I yelled, grabbing her hand. "You want to know? All right, listen."

"Jackson, please." Gaby dropped the spoon. "There's no need to scream."

I rolled my eyes, then started in on the tale. Old book. Important chapter. Dead garden. Blooming roses. Communicate. Infuriate.

"Wait." Juana held up her hand. "Why would a ghost want to haunt Rooter's?"

I squirmed. "Maybe I disturbed its natural sphere or something."

"And digging around, Ro could have disturbed it worse," said Reuben. "The ghost might have started haunting him. That's why Jackson, um, yelled."

"Wow." Gaby's eyes were very bright. "You're going to talk to a ghost."

I shot Juana a glance. "Maybe you should take the kids home."

"No way." Gaby plopped down like a won't-be-budged boulder. "I'm gonna watch."

Reuben shrugged. "The book did say that ghosts sometimes respond to a circle of kindness."

"That's right, a circle of kindness." Gaby crossed her arms.

"I want to be a circle, too," howled Ro.

"Well, come on, then, and quit crying," I said, exasperated. "Hold my—wait! Wipe the worm slime off first."

Ro ran a grubby palm down the front of his T-shirt and grabbed my hand.

"Okay, let's make a circle."

"Jackson," Reuben whispered urgently. "Don't you want to practice first?"

"Practice what?" I said, trying to loosen Ro's slimy grip.

"You know," Reuben continued to whisper. "Your communication."

"Quit *whispering!*" I hollered. "Everyone can hear you—including the ghost."

"I was just trying to help."

"Well, you're making me nervous," I replied. "Here, Ro, wipe your hand again. It feels nasty."

"Circle of kindness, huh," said Gaby, helping her brother. "More like a circle of grouchiness."

If Gaby could infuriate a living, breathing human, think what she'd do to an outlaw-rose ghost.

"Enough." Juana clouted Gaby. "Hold hands, everyone. Listen to Jackson." She gave my hand a go-ahead squeeze.

Slowly we closed our circle round the twig. It looked so ordinary, stuck in the ground. How could it be haunted?

I glanced over my shoulder, checked out the sidewalk. It was bad enough to drive round in a zuke mobile. But if the b-ball guys or Blood saw me chatting up a plant, my cool reputation would be shot forever.

The sidewalk was empty. The air hot and still.

Across from me, Reuben nodded. I tightened my grip on Ro's hand and Juana's.

"Um," I began. "Hello, spirit."

A breeze swirled through. Gaby jumped.

"It's okay," I spoke to the plant. "We're, um, friends. Please don't get mad."

I took a breath. Tried to think what Mama might do. Plants seem to sense feelings, she had told me. And sometimes, she had said, she could sense what they needed. That's how she knew how to help.

"Will the ghost talk?" Gaby whispered.

I closed my eyes. I felt the sun hot on my face and arms. Heard Ro sniff. Smelled the moist dirt turned up by his spoon.

Then a lonesome feeling touched me. Made me shiver.

I opened my eyes.

"You okay?" Juana was peering at me.

Gaby shook my arm. "When's the ghost coming?"

I looked straight at Reuben. "We gotta dig it up," I said. "We gotta bring it back to the cemetery. You were right, man. I'm sorry."

Reuben shrugged. He didn't say "I told

you so." Didn't feed me a gotta-have-respect speech.

"You mean it's over?" Gaby glared first at me, then at Reuben. "No moaning? No chains?"

"What did you expect? A floating sheet?" I smiled over at Reuben. Picked up Ro's spoon. Started to dig.

"Talk about cheap ghosts!" Gaby snorted.

"See if you can find another worm for Ro," Juana said, sifting through the dirt.

"Not from this spot," I said, gently lifting the transplanted twig. "We gotta get this—"

Suddenly a huge hand reached over my shoulder.

The cutting disappeared.

CHAPTER ELEVEN

. . . .

"Aargh," screamed Gaby.

I whirled around.

Blood.

That bully boy took three steps back. Tossed the twig from one flat palm to the other.

"What's this, Rosey Jones?" He dangled the cutting by its skinny roots. "Sure is one *ugly* flower."

"Blood." I took a step closer. "Don't mess with that plant."

"Give it back," ordered Juana.

Blood smirked. "I didn't hear the magic word." His huge fist closed round the twig.

"Please," said Juana.

Blood opened his fist. Yanked a root off the twig.

I lunged—and Blood shoved me back.

"Try that again, Jones, and this thing is dead." His eyes narrowed. "Why you so worried 'bout this stick?"

"We're not," I lied desperately. What if the ghost appeared? What if it was mad?

Gaby pointed at the stick. "Watch out, Blood," she said. "That thing's haunted."

Blood blinked.

"The ghost moans," Gaby whispered spookily. "It rattles chains. And"—she shuddered—"it has no . . . head."

Ro started to cry.

Blood snorted. "You expect me to believe that? I'm gonna tear up this thing—and then get that big baby's worm."

Gaby shrugged. "So, you'll be cursed. Forever. See if we care."

That's when we heard the buzz.

From far off. Just like before.

One huge bee. Gunning for Blood.

That boy dropped the twig and ran.

I heard his feet pounding the sidewalk. Heard his yells.

Then everything went quiet.

After a while, Reuben whispered, "Better pick it up, Jackson."

I reached down. Gently folded the broken twig into my hand.

Slowly we walked to Rooter's gate. As I lifted the latch, Gaby murmured, "You heard me warn him. Now Blood is cursed. Forever."

"He wanted to kill my worm," Ro sniffed.

I glanced back once at the yellow roses. And at the fresh dirt smoothed over the hole left by the twig in my hand. Moist dirt when no one watered the garden. The only roses blooming.

"Jackson," Reuben whispered as the kids and Juana hurried down the sidewalk. "We gotta get that twig back to the cemetery."

"And fast," I agreed.

• • •

But the plant was destined to be in my apartment for another twenty-four hours.

That day it had been dug up, damaged by

Blood, plopped in a cup of water. In the ghost books, spirits often got mad over much, much less. Right now the cutting rested peacefully on the kitchen window ledge. But, as the library book had warned, you never knew with ghosts. Maybe this very minute it was planning the next curse. I bet it could do a LOT of damage in twenty-four hours.

"Jackson, quit pestering." Mama frowned at me over dinner. "You know tomorrow is the first day of the big garden show. I've got a lot of work to do tonight. There's no way I can take you to the country now."

"Please, Mama," I begged.

"If you don't want that cutting," Mama said, "just toss it. No need to drive—"

"NO!" I jumped up. "Promise you won't throw it away, Mama. Promise we'll go to the cemetery tomorrow."

Mama set down her fork. She looked straight at me. "You want to tell me what's going on?"

I did want to tell her. I wanted to lay out the whole ghost story, the curse of the outlaw rose. But something held me back. Mama

59

might try to soothe and heal that cutting. What if, thanks to her gift, it grew and GREW and GREW? What if more folks took cuttings and the ghost got passed around? Fell into evil hands? The wrong person might try to unleash the curse—the poison ivy and bees—upon the city. Or maybe the whole world. Captain Nemo was always fighting villains like that. Or what if scientists wanted to study the plant, like in the experiments Mama had mentioned? They might bombard it with screams and noise. They might chop it into teeny pieces. What if the ghost could never return to its place?

Suddenly that cold, lonesome feeling passed through me again. On the ledge, the cutting trembled.

Yes, the fewer grown-ups who knew about the haunted twig, the better.

"Jackson!" Mama's voice brought me back. "Are you okay?"

I sat back down. "Mama, you just gotta trust me. Tomorrow after the show, we take back the plant. Promise?"

Mama promised, but a worry frown stayed between her eyes.

As we ate, I thought about the twenty-four hours ahead. Reuben and I had planned to spend tomorrow, a Saturday, creating our next Nemo strip. But with the twig around, I drew a big X in my mind through those plans. I didn't want to be in the same building with that haunted thing. I'd be constantly watching for poison ivy and bees. Worrying about my bones. As for my friends, I didn't want them zapped by the curse.

"Can Reuben and I come with you to the garden show?" I spoke up. "Juana, too? And, I suppose, Gaby and Ro?"

"I guess there's enough room in the van," Mama said, surprised. "Oh, let's invite Mr. Kerring. He might enjoy seeing the displays. He's been stuck so long with that broken ankle."

"Sprained," I corrected. "But like Reuben said, an ankle is part of his leg and so the curse—"

I broke off. Luckily, Mama had taken that moment to scrape a plate and hadn't heard.

"Can Mailbags come?" I added.

"Please don't bug that poor man," said Mama. "He has enough to do."

"Mailbags *likes* to be bugged. You know that home for Ro's worm? He made it."

"No."

"No what?"

"No, you can't ask Mailbags. He's busy."

I slumped in my chair. "Well, I call that mean," I grumbled. "Mailbags is always saying nice things about you."

I peeked at Mama, trying some strategy. "He said he would never try to tell you what to do."

"Is that so?" said Mama.

I smiled. "He said it *very* complimentary."

"The man knows a strong mind when he meets one." Mama laughed.

"So?"

"No."

All I can say is, if bees and poison ivy showed up at the apartment building the next day, I hoped Mailbags would be out. And, please, let him avoid all bone-damaging situations.

CHAPTER TWELVE

• •

That ghost gave me the jitters all night long. And all through breakfast, too.

"This is the third time you've jumped up," Mama fussed. "And the third time you've bumped my cup."

"Sorry." I slid back in my seat. "Thought I heard a bee."

"Relax." Mama mopped a coffee spill. "No bee can fly through a closed window."

Except a ghost bee, I thought, remembering Blood's panic the day before. And his puffed-up face a few weeks ago.

"Lord knows I'm jittery, too." Mama sighed, rubbing her finger. "All the money spent rent-ing a booth for the garden show. You've got to advertise for a business to grow. Still, what if no one comes? With the weather so dry—"

"You're scratching," I cried, grabbing her hand. "Poison ivy!"

"Poison ivy in the city?" Mama's worry frown crossed her brow. "You seem awful tense, Jackson. Maybe you should stay home."

With the haunted plant? I jumped up, gathering dishes. "I'll clean the kitchen. You go get ready." I waved her toward the bathroom.

Mama shot me a puzzled look as she left. I turned to the cutting on the ledge. I knew what I had to do.

Mama chatted to plants, encouraging growth. Mr. K. bossed them into bigness. This rose twig needed a different kind of talk.

It needed the facts.

"Listen," I said very firmly. "I know you want to go back to your graveyard."

I waited for the plant, ghost, something to react.

The air was very still.

"This is how it is," I continued. "I promise to

take you tonight. Till then, I don't want any trouble. No broken bones, no bees, no poison ivy. No bad luck for Mama's business. Understand?"

I paused.

There it was again, that cold, lonesome feeling. Making me shiver.

"You miss your home," I spoke softly to the twig. "I'm sorry I moved you."

I stayed by the window for a while, keeping it company.

"You did *what*?" Reuben dropped the watering can with a clatter.

"Careful! That's Mama's display." I grabbed the can by the spout and shoved it into the Green Thumb van. All over again, I explained to Reuben how I had talked to the twig. Sort of the same way the school principal or Mama sometimes talked to me. Slowly. Firmly. No bees. No broken bones. No poison ivy. No trouble. "The ghost understands," I said. "Everything will be fine."

Reuben heaved a doom-and-gloom sigh.

"What?" I said.

"You never know with ghosts," Reuben said in his careful, poke-turtle way. "They're . . . unpredictable."

"Everything will be fine," I repeated.

We finished loading Mama's signs, spades, and shears, and squeezed in beside Gaby, Ro, and Juana. Mama gave an embarrassing *toot-toot* on the horn to Mailbags in his truck, and the zuke mobile was off.

No bees, no broken bones, no poison ivy.

No jitters for me. I felt relaxed all the way to Mr. K.'s building.

Mama pulled up and gave another *toot-toot*.

The door flew open, and out hobbled Mr. K., chased by his nurse. He looked like a skinny gerbil pursued by a stethescope-wearing cat.

"Don't fuss," he barked, scrambling into the front seat. He arranged his cane and waved gleefully to the nurse, who smiled and shook her finger.

"Step on it, Grace," he cried to my mama. "Before the old cat crams another pill down my throat."

The zuke mobile puttered into action,

weaving up the street like a squash stuffed with seeds. Rowdy seeds named Gaby and Ro.

"Ta-da." Mr. K. pulled yellow roses from a brown paper bag.

Small, frilly old-time yellow roses.

The roses the ghost had tended.

"What a beautiful bouquet!" Mama exclaimed.

"A good-luck present for your booth." Mr. K. beamed. "Cut 'em myself this morning. That do-nothing nurse fixed the vase." His gnarly old hands flicked a petal. "Bet those garden-show folks have never seen roses like this."

Good-luck present, ha. Who knew what the ghost might do now?

"Speaking of roses, Jackson." Mr. K. suddenly turned to me. "How's that cutting from the cemetery? Have you planted it at Rooter's?"

Reuben and I exchanged glances. In all the worry about the ghost, we had completely forgotten our reason for clipping the rose twig in the first place. Mr. K.: rose rustler.

"Speak up, boy." Mr. K. frowned. "How's that cutting?"

Luckily, at that moment, a terrible stink distracted the man.

"Ro!" Juana complained.

"But my worm is lonely," whined Ro. "Let me talk to him. Just for a minute."

"The lid goes on *now*," Juana ordered.

Quickly Mama let down the windows and we gulped city air.

"See what I have to live with?" Gaby moaned. "A rotten worm."

"He's healthy," Ro assured her. "He's just making—"

"We know," said Juana.

Ro mournfully stuck his thumb in his mouth. "My worm needs a friend," he murmured.

I closed my eyes against the hot breeze from the window. Saved by a worm. Maybe Mr. K. would forget about the cutting, at least till we had returned it to the cemetery. Then it would be too late for him to plant it at Rooter's himself—and to try bossing it into growth. Now I had a ghost *and* Mr. K. to deal with. Talk about stress. *No bees, no broken bones, no poison ivy.* I made a silent song with the words. *No questions from Mr. K.*

"Oh, look," Mama called. "Isn't that Howard Green? But what's he doing?"

"Strange boy," barked Mr. K.

My eyes snapped open.

Blood was scurrying down the sidewalk. Not swaggering. Not sauntering. *Scurrying.* His head swiveled constantly. Right, left, up, down.

"Maybe he's searching for something." Mama slowed the van, *toot-toot*ed the horn at Blood. "Can we help?"

Blood glanced at the zuke mobile. His eyes locked on mine. Widened with fear.

Then he bolted down the sidewalk.

"Look at him go," Mr. K. said admiringly. "Big—but he runs like a deer."

"Did you see the bee?" Reuben whispered.

Juana shook her head. "But the way Blood is acting, he must be listening for it," she whispered back.

I got a mind picture of Blood's face. Scared. Constantly searching. Waiting for that bee to strike. Yeah, maybe that bee was giving Blood a bit of what he'd been giving other kids for years.

"That poor boy," Mama murmured. "He looked so scared. Maybe we should follow—"

"Won't do any good," Gaby declared from the back. "He's cursed."

"Cursed?"

"Haunted by a ghost," Gaby explained loudly while we tried to shush her. "And it serves him right."

"He tried to kill my worm," Ro spoke up.

"Ghosts? Nonsense!" Mr. K. snorted. "That's the trouble with kids today. Too much imagination."

CHAPTER THIRTEEN

•••••••••••••••••••••••

No bees, no broken bones, no poison ivy, I sang silently all the way to the garden show. *No questions from Mr. K. No bad business for Mama.*

Those words sang through my mind while we unloaded Mama's signs and spades and Ro's stinky worm.

But when we stumbled through the convention center door, my singing suddenly stopped.

"A-ma-zing," murmured Reuben.

An indoor garden spread before me. The scene was as pretty as one of Mama's magazines. Bright as Oz in the movie.

I stared. The garden stretching over the huge floor was actually made up of many little gardens. Like Rooter's, but without weeds. Pansies lined teeny lawns as smooth as green felt. Lilies raised high their trumpet flowers. Fountains trickled and tinkled a watery music. No waterfalls, though, probably due to the drought.

Everything was lined up just so, the way Mr. K. liked his plot. But the old man snorted when he read the sign on a gleaming bench. FOR DISPLAY ONLY. "Fancy-pants garden," he barked. "No place to sit."

"Come help me set up." Mama took his arm kindly. "You can man my booth."

Though small, Mama's booth managed to look "festive" (her word) once we set out the spades and hung the Green Thumb signs. Reuben arranged Mama's business cards on a table.

"Those yellow roses sure catch the eye." Mr. K. nodded at the vase beside them.

We lined up across the front of the booth, ready for business. Gaby smoothed Ro's hair.

72

"Keep the lid on that worm," she advised. "Or the stink will drive off customers."

"My worm's gonna help." Ro smiled serenely.

Mama surveyed our line. "Could be there's more helpers than booth space. Why don't you take turns?"

Of course, Gaby, Ro, and the worm disappeared immediately, with Juana in pursuit. Reuben wandered off to sketch; Mr. K. had to hunt down the bathroom. Finally, Mama asked if she could attend a class on arranging cattails.

"Go," I said.

And that's how I found myself an hour later, the only man manning the booth.

I leaned back in the metal chair. Ah, I felt as fine as a big-shot business guy. I chatted to the lady in the next booth, who gave me a tulip-shaped pot holder. I straightened Mama's business cards. This time the next day, the haunted rose twig would be back in its proper place. No more trouble. "You look great," I murmured to Mr. K.'s yellow blooms.

Suddenly a voice boomed: "Young man!"

I jumped. *Whoosh* went the vase. Water all over. I grabbed the pot holder, frantically mopped.

"Young man," the voice boomed again, "where did you get those roses?"

CHAPTER FOURTEEN

• •

I felt like an outlaw for sure. "I didn't st-
steal them," I stammered. "Mr. K. took them.
From his garden, I mean. He gave them to my
mother."

"Where is your mother?"

The man loomed over me. His gray eye-
brows bristled like two caterpillars.

"Where is your mother?" he repeated,
scooping up a soggy flower.

The curse was reaching beyond the garden.
Would Mama and Mr. K. get in trouble?

"Those roses came from Texas," I rushed to
explain. "In a potato. A long time ago."

"What's the name?"

"JACKSON!"

Ro rounded a corner, raced for the booth. "GUESS WHAT?"

"Hey, the floor's wet." Gaby slid to a halt beside her brother. "And so are your mama's cards! Boy, will she be mad."

"JACKSON!" Ro tugged at my shirt.

"Don't pay any attention to him," Gaby informed the man. "He's excited 'cause—hey, who are you?"

"I'm a judge."

"Like Judge Judy on TV?" Gaby asked. "Do you put people in jail?"

The man chuckled. "Actually, I'm a judge of—"

"WORMS." Ro continued tugging. "Come see, Jackson."

"He found a worm farm." Gaby sighed.

"Oh, those are great." The man's cater-brows wagged happily. "I have a little one."

"Are you a worm judge?"

"Roses," said the man.

"Well, anyway, *please* tell my brother an important fact: Worms are NOT pets."

Ro beamed. "My worm will have *hundreds* of friends," he said.

"Indeed," said the man, looking confused.

He waved the yellow rose at me, scattering drops. "May I take this, young man?"

Gaby perked up. "What for?"

"I want to identify it."

"We'll sell it to you," said Gaby.

"Shhh." I poked her, then turned back to the man. "I guess you can take it. But why?"

The man's brows wagged again. "I can't make any promises," he murmured, "but this rose may be rare. Very rare." He wiped one of Mama's wet business cards on his shirt and tucked it into his pocket. "I'll call when I find out."

"Jackson," Gaby wailed as the man strode down the aisle. "You let him *steal* your mama's flower. Five bucks down the drain. Maybe ten. I bet we *never* see that man again."

• • •

Mama said pretty much the same thing when I told her the whole story. "We'll probably never hear from that man," she said as we headed home in the zuke mobile. "What could he possibly discover?"

"Nothing fancy-pants about that rose,"

Mr. K. barked. "Good, hardy stock. My grand-mother brought the cutting from Texas. In a potato!"

"I mentioned that to the judge," I said.

Mama hummed as she drove. Lots of folks had stopped by and picked up her (wet) business cards. Ro hummed to his worm, now tucked in a non-stinky farm with some wiggly friends. The small contraption was a present from Mr. K. "You can start your own business," he had told the little boy. "I'll buy your worms for my plot."

Business? Gaby IMMEDIATELY got involved. Miss CEO announced she would help feed the worms for a cut of the profits.

I hoped to be humming soon. The haunted plant preyed on my mind. I had promised to take it back to the graveyard after the show. I couldn't rest till then.

No bees, no broken bones, no poison ivy. No trouble. Those words sang in my head all the way home. All the way to where that rose twig waited for me.

Chapter Fifteen

• •

At six o'clock, that twig was still waiting.

The zuke mobile had made a looonnng stop at the Space Shuttle Grill. Mama wanted to treat everyone to ice cream for helping with her booth.

The Space Shuttle is my favorite eat-out place in the city. The ice cream is served in flying saucers. It's where Reuben and I had come up with the brilliant idea to create Captain Nemo.

But right then, my man and I had places to go. Namely a graveyard.

Of course, Gaby decided to chew each mouthful twenty-nine times. So did Ro.

"You don't *chew* ice cream," I said.

"Chewing well is good for your digestion," she replied, all prissy.

"Enjoy the quiet," Juana advised me, scraping her bowl. "Chewing keeps 'em busy."

I tried to hurry things along. "Look, Mama!" I flung my arm toward the window. "The sun's going down."

"The sun goes down every day," Mama grumbled, mopping a soda spill. "See, you knocked my cup again. What's got you so jittery now? Another bee?"

"It's getting *dark*."

Reuben shot me a worried look. My man and I were sharing the same thought, for sure. It was bad enough to haul a ghost plant to a graveyard. We didn't want to do it at night.

"Oh, Jackson," Mama sighed. "Can't the planting wait till tomorrow?"

"NO," Reuben and I both shouted.

"Your mama's tired, boy," Mr. K. barked. "Of course the planting can wait."

Luckily, Mr. K. seemed fixed more on postponing the planting than on what was being planted. We had to get that cutting to the graveyard *fast*. Haunted twig? Rose ghost? He'd never believe us.

"Mama, you *promised*," I pleaded.

And I had promised the twig. If I broke that promise, no telling what the ghost might do.

"You seen the bee lately?" Reuben whispered.

"Thought I heard it at breakfast," I whispered back. "You think it's a warning?"

Reuben moaned.

"Does your stomach hurt? Can I have your ice cream?" Gaby grabbed Reuben's bowl. Ro grabbed mine.

They both commenced spooning. Chewing. One . . . two . . . three . . .

• • •

"Oof." Gaby FINALLY pushed away Reuben's bowl. "I'm full."

Ro jiggled the worm farm. "My guys want to go home."

FINALLY we piled into the zuke mobile

again. Stopped before our apartment building. I ran in, grabbed the twig, ran out. . . . That's when I discovered the chew-counting duo were bailing.

"My worms are sleepy," Ro explained.

"You're scared." I crossed my arms. "You don't want to go to the graveyard."

"Do you?" asked Gaby.

Well, no. But I also didn't want that haunted twig in my home another hour, another minute, another second.

"Chicken," I said.

"Cluck, cluck," said Gaby.

"Sorry, Jackson." Juana followed the little kids out of the van. "I gotta keep them out of trouble."

That left Mama, Mr. K., Reuben, me.

My man and I needed to get rid of Mr. K. before he got us in trouble—with the ghost.

"Mr. Kerring," Reuben spoke up politely. "You must be awful tired."

"Yes," I agreed, even more politely. "We can drop you off right now, before we go—"

"Tired? Me?" The old man trained his sharp

eyes on us. "Nonsense! By the way, where *are* you going?"

"Um," said Reuben.

"Um," I repeated.

"The boys suggested a little drive to the country," Mama cut in. "You know, to enjoy the late-spring evening."

"They did, huh?" The old man smiled. "Why, I believe I'll go, too." He settled deeper into his seat. "Nothing for me at home but that nurse."

I sighed. Please, no more questions. No probing into exactly why we suggested a drive to the country. Despite all his "nonsense" talk, Mr. K. did look tired. Maybe he'd fall asleep.

Reuben nodded solemnly at me. I hoped we could take on a ghost. Especially an impatient one.

The time: seven o'clock.

• • •

Mr. K.'s head bobbed and bounced and finally drooped in sleep. Mama drove slowly, taking in the country landscape and giving out a few teachable moments. She pointed out the difference between a Holstein cow and an Angus bull. Identified a blackberry thicket. Exclaimed over the dry leaves on a giant oak. "We need rain," she said. "How many days has it been?"

"Twenty-eight," said Reuben.

Soon Mama was trotting out tales of her country childhood. How she had tended strawberries in the garden. Snapped beans on the porch. Explored fields on her very own horse.

The animal's name? Jackson. That's right, I was named for a horse.

Talk about embarrassing. But this is how I figure it: Mama had so much love wrapped up in the land and that four-legged creature that she needed to put it *somewhere* when she moved to the city. So she had transplanted those feelings to her houseplants and kid.

It could have been worse. What if she'd loved a cow?

Mama's country talk rolled right over

Reuben and me. We were focused on the twig. It rested quietly between us on the backseat. So far, so good. I thought of that twig returning to the graveyard, returning to the other pink roses twining on the old fence.

"The old fence," I whispered.

Reuben shot me a scared look. I could tell my man and I were sharing one bad, BAD thought.

On our first trip to the graveyard, the clean-up manager had said his crew planned to tear down the old fence and cut away growth. What if the fence was gone? And the pink roses, too? What if there was no place for the cutting to return to?

What might the ghost do then?

In the front, Mr. K. dozed, softly snoring.

Smack! Something struck the windshield.

"Did you see that bee?" Mama peered out her window. "Huge! And it flew off, like it wasn't hurt."

Once again my mind started its singing: *No bees, no broken bones, no poison ivy.* I added another song: *Please, please, PLEASE let the fence be okay.*

"Miz Jones"—Reuben was polite but grim—
"you gotta drive faster."

FINALLY Mama found the path that led
from the road into the woods. The path that
we'd followed to the graveyard. She parked
the van. Handed me the flashlight from the
glove compartment.

Twilight had settled like a gray sheet over
everything.

"Are you sure you need to do this?" she
asked, giving me the eye.

I nodded. Reuben hoisted a spade.

"Well, if you're not back in twenty minutes,"
she said, "I'm going after you."

Mr. K. continued to snore. Reuben and I
softly closed the van door. Took our first
steps along the path. The woods swallowed
us immediately. When I turned, I couldn't see
the zuke mobile.

I switched on the flashlight. The beam
bounced ahead. It lit the dull needles droop-
ing from pines, the cracked leaves of a
sycamore. Twigs snapped underfoot. The
drought had drained the life from everything.
I could smell the hot dryness. One spark from

a match or lightning and *whoosh*. The whole forest would go up in flames.

Suddenly Reuben stumbled into me.

"Sorry, man," he said. "Thought I saw—"

Bzzzz. A giant bee hovered before us. Blood's bee.

Chapter Sixteen

• •

I clutched the twig. Felt its wiry strength.

The bee's buzz filled the air.

"J-Jackson, look," chattered Reuben.

He pointed to some large gray blobs in the darkness. I swept the flashlight beam and, in the light, saw the graveyard. The hulking stones.

And the old fence . . . covered with roses.

That meant the broken-bone-poison-ivy-bee-sting curse had scared off the clean-up crew.

Staring at the roses, I shivered. Every plant in that forest was dry and dying. But those roses . . . soft and full. Like someone tended them carefully. Watered them once a day.

"L-like Mr. K.'s yellow roses," whispered Reuben.

The big bee swooped toward the fence, circled back. Buzzed.

I steeled myself for the sting.

"Hey," said Reuben. "I think it wants us to follow."

The bee swooped off again. Circled back.

And wouldn't you know, it buzzed us straight to the stone closest to the fence. The gravestone that had tripped me. Straight to the place where I had taken the cutting.

Reuben and I knew just what to do. We dropped to our knees and dug.

We stuck that twig in the hole, tamped down the earth.

"Let's get out of here," Reuben panted.

But something held me. I breathed in the night, filled with rose smell. Felt the weight and age of the surrounding trees. I touched the stone beside the twig. Squinted at the letters revealed by the flashlight.

"Rose . . . Cassoway," Reuben read aloud. "Can't make out the dates, though."

I bounced the beam off the other gravestones.

Read the writing below the names: BELOVED HUSBAND . . . SADLY MOURNED.

"Rose's stone is smaller than the others," murmured Reuben.

Well, it is hard to make a circle of kindness with just two people. But it can be done. I apologized to Rose for disturbing her spot, for cutting her flowers. I wished her peace. So did Reuben.

When we left, I turned round just once. The roses glowed in the darkness. And that bee . . . I swear, that bee was swooping and buzzing around them. Watching over them even at night.

• • •

When we returned to the van, Mama's worry frown was between her eyes. "You okay?"

I nodded, too tired to answer.

Mr. K. was wide awake and full of questions. "Your mama said you returned the rose cutting to the cemetery. Why?"

"It wasn't happy at Rooter's," I murmured, sliding into my seat.

"Happy?" he barked. "Nonsense! A plant either grows or it doesn't. If it doesn't, throw—"

"But then we would have missed this drive to the country." Mama nodded at me and pointed to tiny flicks of light in the darkness. "Look, fireflies!"

Mr. K. humphed, but I caught his sudden smile.

Mama started the van and swung onto the road. "Those cemetery roses are probably old-fashioned, like the yellow ones," she said. "Even if the cutting didn't grow at Rooter's, do you think the rose judge might be interested?"

"No," I said firmly.

Luckily, Mr. K. picked that moment to launch a lecture. "Nothing fancy-pants about old-time roses." He snorted. "Judges like la-de-da modern hybrids. Big petals and no smell. Del-i-cate. Mark my words, you'll never hear from the man."

Mr. K. loved his lecture. His voice grew louder. "I ever tell you how my grandmother brought that yellow-rose cutting from Texas?"

Reuben and I nodded.

"Stuck in a potato," he happily continued. "Yup, those yellow roses are tough. They can survive drought and blight. Look how they lasted this spring when everything else shriveled up. Huh, they can grow in *shade,* when most roses need sun. Why, one kind of Texas rose even lived through a fire."

I tried not to yawn.

"Mind you, I never actually *saw* that rosebush. Couldn't tell you if the blooms were white, red, or pink. My grandmother told me the story. See, she had a friend come up from Texas about the same time she did. The woman—no more'n a girl, really—brought a cutting, too. To listen to my gran, this girl had the gift. She'd set a stick in soil . . . the next day, flowers."

Reuben slumped beside me. My eyes closed sleepily.

"My grandmother couldn't wait to leave Texas, that dry, dusty place. But her friend called that big state home. The husband, though, wanted to try his luck in the East, and so she came, bringing their baby. Settled somewhere around here."

The zuke mobile hummed down the highway. The darkness cozied in.

"—lost everything in that fire. House, husband. Little girl, too. Buried what remained of the bodies. Left her roses behind. In a few weeks, she was back in Texas."

"Oh, that poor woman," Mama murmured.

"Wish I could remember the name," Mr. K. droned. "Cassovava? Cassovara?"

My eyes snapped open.

"Cassoway?" Reuben spoke up.

"Maybe," said Mr. K. "I can't recall. She had an outlandish first name, though."

"Rose?" I whispered.

Mr. K swiveled round to glare at me. "What you whispering for, boy? My hearing's bad enough. Did you say 'Rose'?" He paused. Shook his head. "I can't recall. No, seems Rose was the name of the little girl. A silly business, naming children for flowers."

"I named a boy for a horse." Mama winked at me in the rearview mirror.

Mr. K. slapped his knee. "Oooh, Jackson," he laughed, "what if that horse was called Daisy?"

I smiled but kept quiet. In the darkness, I thought of that young woman. She had lost everything: home and husband and child. Her love—where had it gone? It had gotten transplanted, maybe. Maybe to roses. Was she trying still to protect them? Maybe her ghost, shaped like a bee, watched over the grave of her daughter and the roses that grew there.

I thought and thought as the van rolled home. And then I must have slept.

CHAPTER SEVENTEEN
....

So was the curse lifted? The curse of the out-law rose?

Was there even a curse to begin with?

I don't know.

I do know three things.

Number one: The judge guy did call. Turned out the yellow rose *was* rare. It was an "antique" and had never been named. The man explained that it should be registered, so other folks could learn about it. Thanks to his grandmother, the rose belonged to Mr. K., but he asked Reuben and me to do the honors.

Gaby voted for Gabrielle Marie. Of course, she contributed her own name.

Reuben suggested The Nemo, for our space-comic hero.

Mailbags showed Reuben and me a rose book from the library. There was page after page of long, prissy names. Europena, French Lace, Fortune's Double Yellow. Many roses were named for the people who had found or first grown them.

Because of Blood and his "Flower Boy" taunts, I knew I didn't want a rose with my name.

"What about the name of a place?" asked Mailbags.

So we called it Rooter's. Rooter's Rose. "A good name for a sturdy rose," Mr. K. said approvingly.

• • •

The second thing I know: The day after we returned the twig, the skies sent rain. Not roaring thunder or lightning. Not slashing, smashing drops. Just a steady downpour that soaked the earth and brought green back to the garden.

A coincidence? Of course. Nothing super-natural about a drought.

• • •

The third thing? Blood quit being a BIG bully. Mind you, he was still a little bully. He'd let loose a "Rose Jones" or "Art Fart" every once in a while, but he laid off the punching, pounding, and stealing. And if a bee buzzed near—even a gentle bumble guy—Blood would leave *fast.* Maybe being haunted had given his mean self a feeling for the fear and pain of other kids. Or maybe, as Gaby said, the boy believed he was cursed. Forever.

• • •

One mystery remained, though. How had Mama, Reuben, and I escaped the curse? I had cut the graveyard twig. Reuben had touched it many times. It had lived with Mama and me. And yet we had remained un-hurt. No poison ivy, no bee stings, no broken bones.

For weeks, Reuben and I tried to puzzle it

out. And one July day, while we lollygagged at Rooter's, Reuben hit on a possible reason.

"Maybe the twig didn't hurt us," he explained, "because we didn't try to hurt it."

"Go on." I plucked a grass blade from under my puddle of thorns.

"Think about it," said Reuben. "The clean-up crew at the cemetery, the manager with the beard, Blood—everyone wanted to destroy it."

"But I cut the twig and took it away."

"You were going to plant it," Reuben said. "You were helping that rose to live."

I blew a nice, screechy whistle on the grass blade. "But Mr. K. wasn't doing any damage," I pointed out. "And he sprained his ankle."

Reuben smiled. "I bet Mr. K. got bossy. You know, *commanding* that twig to grow."

Mama had said that plants can sense feelings. Maybe the outlaw rose had flat-out refused to live with that bossy man—and had taken action. Huh, that was one *spooky* twig.

Or was it?

"Reuben." I fiddled with a thorn on my rose bush. "Do you *really* believe that twig was haunted? I mean, Mr. K. said those old-time roses could live a long time with no rain. And he said they could survive in shade, which explains why the graveyard roses could grow in a forest. Maybe everything that happened was, well, *normal.* No ghosts involved."

My man took a looonnng, poke-turtle slow time pulling a weed.

I shivered. "But then I remember the feeling that sometimes came off that plant. That sad lonesomeness. How do you explain that?"

Maybe we would never know for sure. Pulling weeds, though, Reuben and I came to one important conclusion. "Haunted twig," "outlaw rose"—that plant needed a less scary name.

From that day on, we called it the Cassoway Rose. Only to ourselves, though. We would never tell the rose judge, even though the Cassoway was probably rare. We wouldn't register it. We would leave it alone in the graveyard, watched over by the bee.

Who knew, though? Maybe the mama ghost bee (the pink-rose guardian) would visit Rooter's sometime. She'd want to check on Mr. K.'s old-time yellow roses, after giving them so much care.

"Listen, Reuben." I whistled another grass blade. "We need a good villain for the next Nemo strip. One with thorns, maybe."

My man considered the idea. "Giant thorns," he added.

"Filled with poison."

As we planned the ultimate fight between Nemo and the evil Thorngruber, I realized a fourth thing I was starting to know. For the first time in my life, maybe roses had not been bad luck.

AUTHOR'S NOTE

If a house can be haunted, why not a garden? After all, many antique roses, dating to before 1867, are being found these days at abandoned houses and old cemeteries, the usual territory for ghosts. An article on rose rustling in *Smithsonian Magazine* first pricked my interest in finding and preserving old-fashioned roses. These roses tend to be smaller, sweeter-smelling, and hardier than roses grown since 1867—the year when hybrids, raised for size and thick-petaled beauty, were first introduced. In a way, old roses are a bit of living history. They continue to thrive in many historic gardens and still grow in many backyards. Why, your great-great-great-great-grandparents may have sniffed an Old Blush on a summer day.

ABOUT THE AUTHOR

Mary Quattlebaum is an award-winning author of picture books, poetry, and novels for children, including two companions to *Jackson Jones and the Curse of the Outlaw Rose*. *Jackson Jones and the Puddle of Thorns* won the Marguerite de Angeli Prize and a *Parenting* Reading Magic Award, and *Jackson Jones and Mission Greentop* was praised by *The Bulletin of the Center for Children's Books* as "a spirited tale . . . of youthful activism" with an "easygoing, everykid voice." Mary Quattlebaum has worked as an eighteenth-century-costumed waitress for Colonial Williamsburg, as director of a poetry and family folklore program, and as medical writer for a children's hospital. She now writes frequently for the *Washington Post* and teaches creative writing in Washington, D.C., where she lives with her family. For years Mary Quattlebaum tended a plot in a city community garden, where she found many weeds—but never a haunted rose.

You can read more about the author and her books at www.maryquattlebaum.com.